KT-379-591

THIS BOOK BELONGS TO

.....

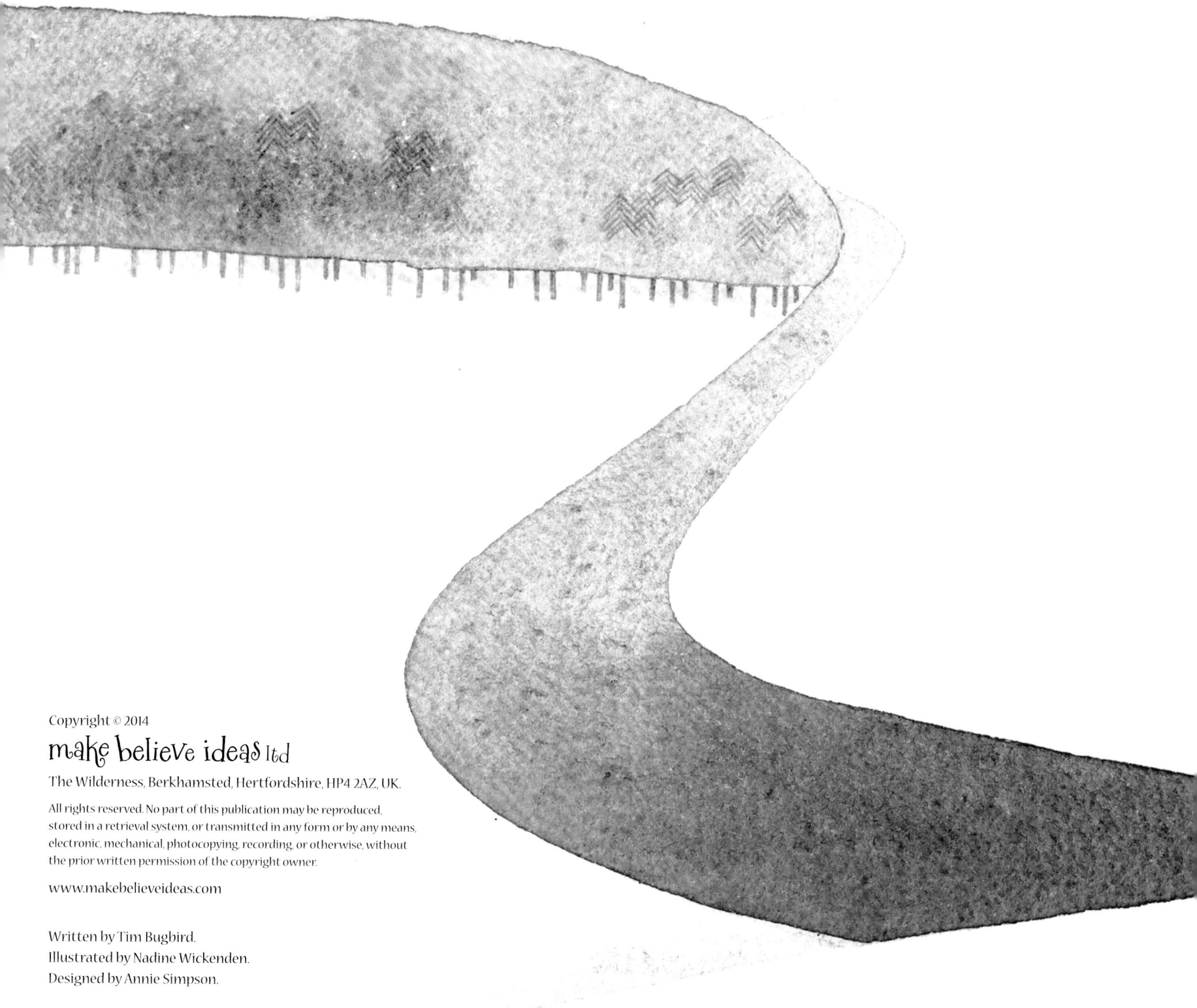

Copyright © 2014

make believe ideas ltd

The Wilderness, Berkhamsted, Hertfordshire, HP4 2AZ, UK.

All rights reserved. No part of this publication may be reproduced, stored in a retrieval system, or transmitted in any form or by any means, electronic, mechanical, photocopying, recording, or otherwise, without the prior written permission of the copyright owner.

www.makebelieveideas.com

Written by Tim Bugbird.
Illustrated by Nadine Wickenden.
Designed by Annie Simpson.

The Perfect Gift

Tim Bugbird • Nadine Wickenden

make believe ideas

Three days before Christmas,
Little Squeak was playing
in the forest when he
saw a beautiful acorn.
"This will be the perfect gift
for Big," he thought.

Little Squeak carefully wrapped the acorn in a golden leaf and hid it in the hollow of an old tree trunk.

On Christmas Eve, Little Squeak collected the acorn.
But just moments from home, it slipped from his paws,
rolled into the stream and was washed away.

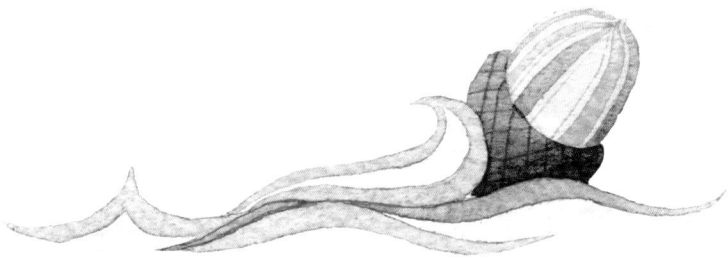

"I'm sorry," he said to Big.
"I lost your gift and have nothing
to give you for Christmas."

"But you have already given me so much!" replied Big.
"Dry your tears and I'll explain . . ."

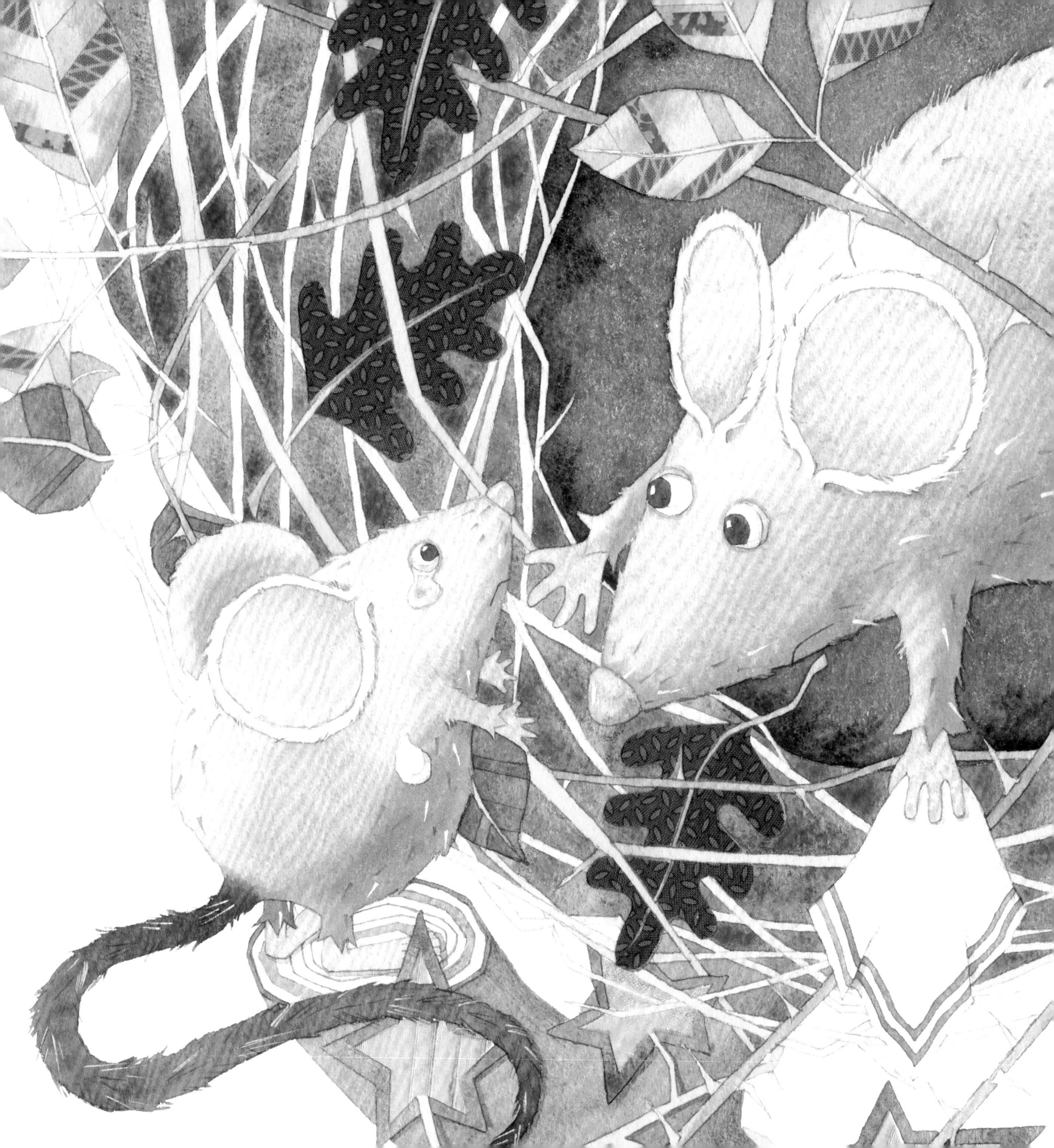

The gift you give has no shape or size.
It's the love that I see
when I look in
your eyes.

It's the way that you *laugh*

when I tickle your *toes*...

and the smile

on my face

when you wrinkle

your nose.

It's not tied with ribbons

and it doesn't

look grand.

It's the **trust** that you give

when you take my **hand.**

Your **gift** isn't fancy,

but inside, it glows **bright.**

It's the **warmth**

that I feel when we

cuddle up tight.

It's **beautiful** music – my own special sound.

It's the **song** in my **heart**

when you are around.

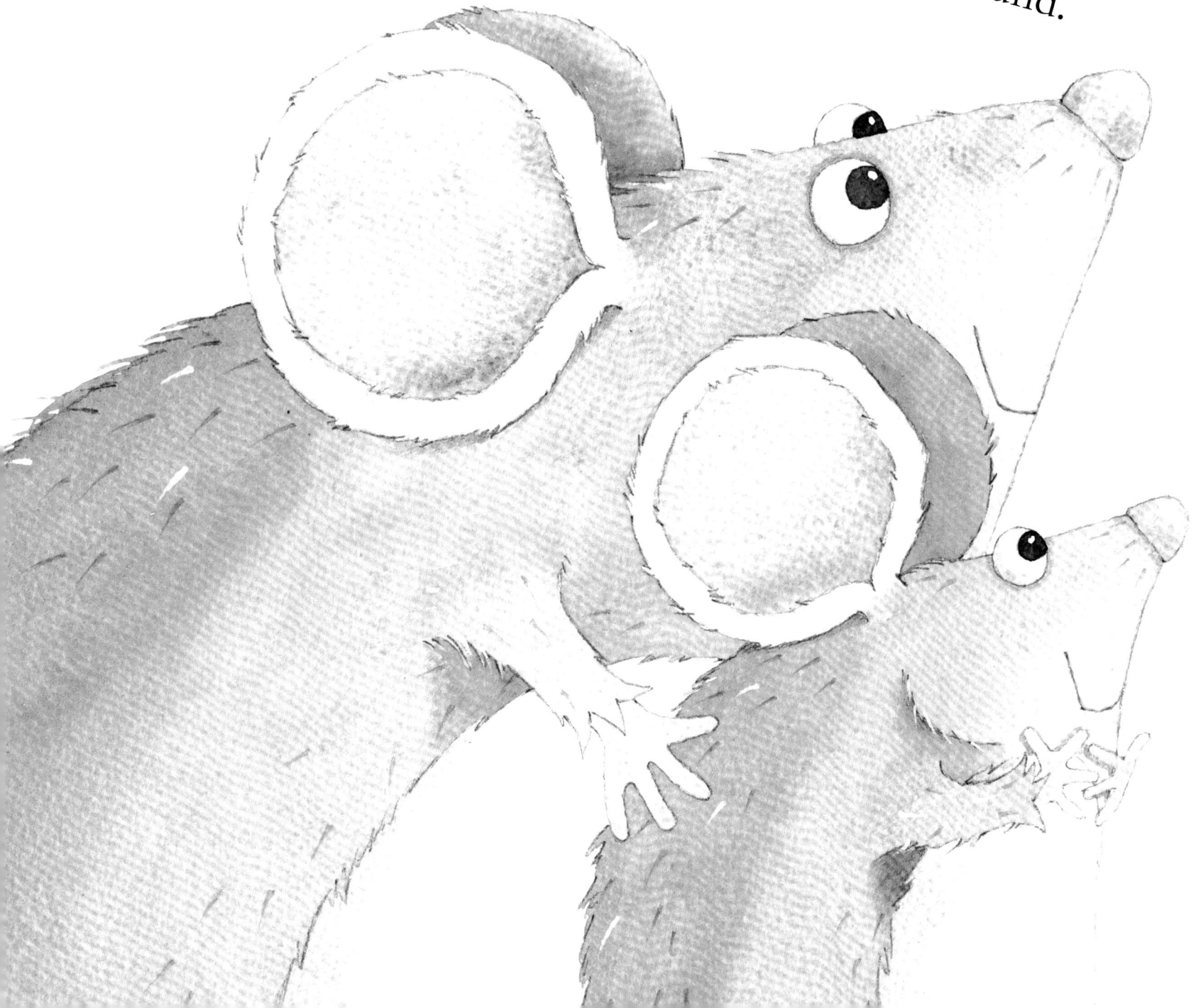

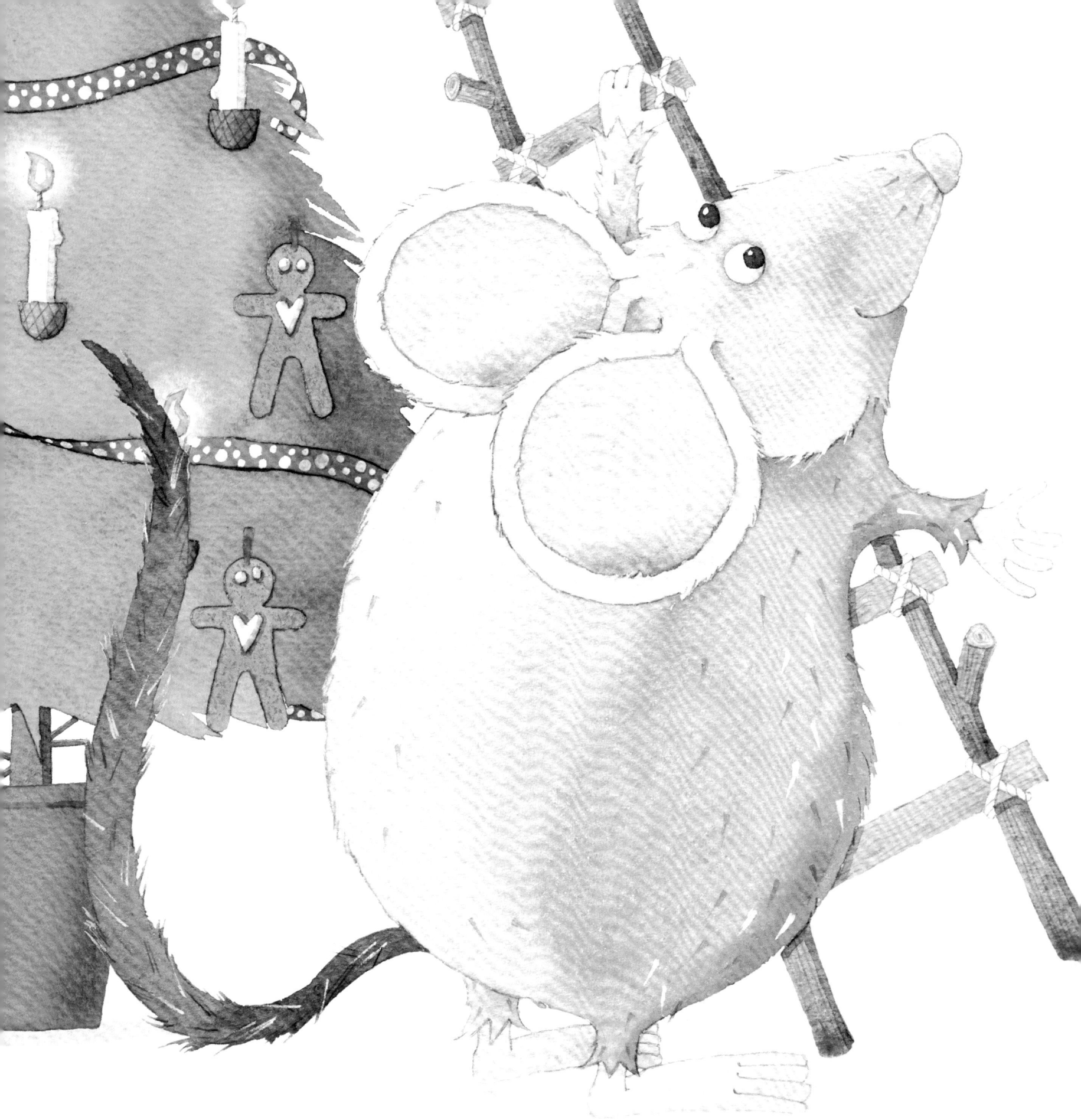

When you've only one left, but say,

"This is yours,"

you give me **much more**

than is held in your paws.

And as time passes by, it's a **gift** to know

I'll receive such **joy**

just watching you **grow.**

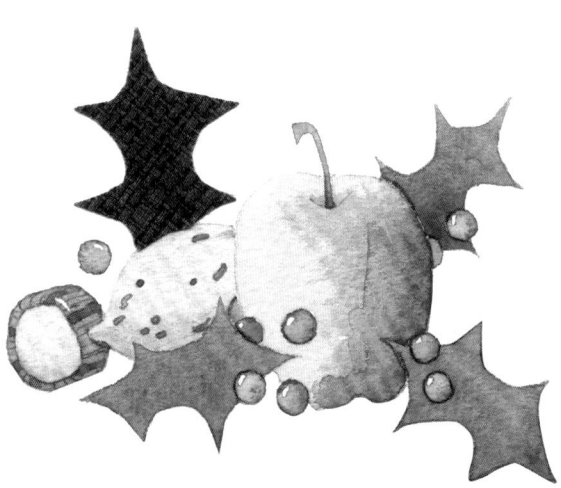

6
5
4
3
2

So we'll hang up our stockings,

but remember what's true . . .

I have **all**

that I need;

the **perfect gift**

is **you!**

In the distance, a clock struck twelve; it was Christmas Day.

Little Squeak and Big looked up at the stars.
"Thank you," said Little Squeak.

"Thank you," said Big.

THE END